Dinos Are Forever

Greg Trine

Art by Frank W. Dormer

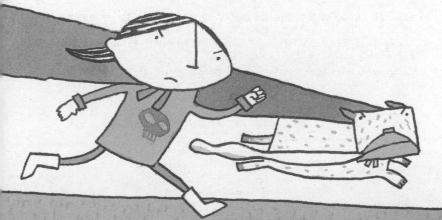

Houghton Mifflin Harcourt
Boston New York

For information about permission to reproduce selections from this book, write to
trade.permissions@hmhco.com or to Permissions, Houghton Mifflin Harcourt
Publishing Company, 3 Park Avenue, 19th Floor, New York, New York 10016.

www.hmhco.com

The text of this book is set in Adobe Garamond and King Cool KC Pro.

The Library of Congress has cataloged the hardcover edition as follows:
Trine, Greg.
Dinos are forever / written by Greg Trine and illustrated by Frank W. Dormer.
p. cm.
[1. Superheroes—Fiction. 2. Grandfathers—Fiction. 3. Dogs—Fiction. 4.
Middle schools—Fiction. 5. Schools—Fiction. 6. San Francisco (Calif.)—Fic-
tion. 7. Humorous stories.]
I. Dormer, Frank W., ill. II. Title.
PZ7.T7356Din 2012   [E]—dc23   2011041933

ISBN 978-0-547-76341-5 hardcover
ISBN 978-0-544-00325-5 paperback

Printed in the United States of America
DOC 10 9 8 7
4500758297

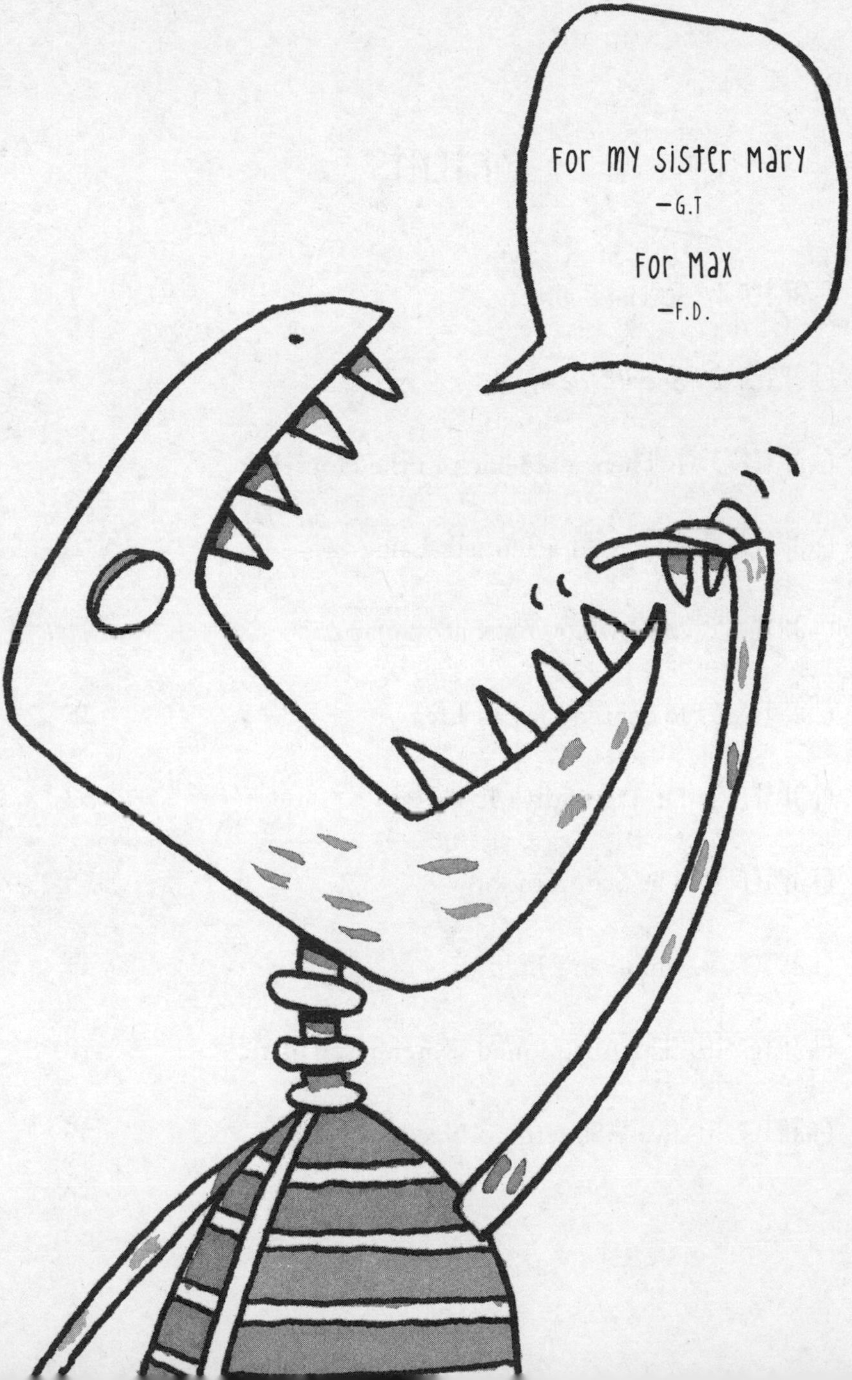
For my sister Mary
—G.T
For Max
—F.D.

contents

Chapter 1: Special Delivery   1

Chapter 2: Sheriff Joe   7

Chapter 3: Is There a Sidekick in the House?   12

Chapter 4: The Mad Scientist's Lair   16

Chapter 5: Meanwhile, Back at the Jacuzzi   21

Chapter 6: Jo Schmo Has an Idea   28

Chapter 7: Dr. Dastardly's Evil Plan   32

Chapter 8: The Schmomobile   35

Chapter 9: Simon and Ralph   41

Chapter 10: The Abandoned Warehouse District   48

Chapter 11: Every Superhero Needs a Hideout   55

Chapter 12: Dr. Dastardly 60

Chapter 13: Knuckle Sandwich . . . on Rye 64

Chapter 14: *Mwah-ha-ha!* 70

Chapter 15: The Re-animator Laminator 75

Chapter 16: *ZAP!* 79

Chapter 17: Volkswagens, Chevys, and Fords, Oh My! 85

Chapter 18: Halt Because I Said So! 88

Chapter 19: Put Me Down! 93

Chapter 20: Jo and Raymond to the Rescue 97

Chapter 21: Lofty Thoughts 101

1

Special Delivery

Jo Schmo came from a long line of crime fighters. She knew that one day she too would wear a badge. But for now she was content to live the life of a normal fourth grade girl and do normal fourth grade things.

Like riding her motorized skateboard.

And trying to figure out which boys she had crushes on. It wasn't easy. There were so many to choose from. It was only the first week of school, and already she'd made some pretty important decisions:

Kevin had the best hair.

Mitch looked spectacular in green.

David had exactly seventeen freckles, which she absolutely adored.

And that was just the beginning. She was also fairly certain that she liked Tom, Dick, and Harry.

Skateboards and crushes—this was Jo Schmo's life. At least it was before the mysterious package arrived.

She knew it was a mysterious package for two reasons. First, that was what the deliveryman called it. "Mysterious package for Jo," he announced.

"Jo who?" Jo asked.

"Jo Schmo."

Jo's grandpa Joe lived in a shack behind the house. When someone asked for "Jo," maybe they meant "Joe." You had to find out which Jo it was—Jo or Joe.

This time it was Jo.

"That's me," Jo said to the deliveryman, and she took the package.

The second reason she knew it was a mysterious package was the writing on the package itself.

Mysterious Package for:
Jo Schmo
4893 Crimshaw Avenue
San Francisco, CA 94102

"Mysterious package," Jo said. She held it out for her dog, Raymond, to sniff. You couldn't be too careful about mysterious packages. It could be a bomb. On TV, dogs were always sniffing for bombs. Raymond gave the package the once-over with his nose, then looked at Jo in a way that said, "I detect snacks. Open it at once."

Jo tore open the package. Inside she found not

snacks, but a red cape and a note from her uncle George.

"I have an uncle George?" Jo asked her mom, who was standing nearby.

Her mother nodded. "Yes, but really he's my second cousin once removed."

"Why was he removed?"

"We used to call him Stinky George. Need I say more?" her mother said.

"Nope. I get the picture."

"Good," her mother said, wrinkling her nose. She hadn't heard from Uncle George in years. Nor had she smelled him. Which was kind of a good thing, if you think about it.

Jo turned back to the note from her uncle.

Dear Jo,

I am retiring from my life as a superhero and have enclosed my cape. Use it well.

Sincerely,

Uncle George

"Hmm . . ." Jo said. Her uncle was a superhero? *Use it well?* As in "Put on the cape and catch bad guys"? Just yesterday she'd written love letters to Tom, Dick, and Harry. Then again, fighting crime did run in her family. Jo Schmo, Crime Fighter, did have a certain ring to it. But Jo Schmo, Superhero?

Could she really stop trains and fly? Could she really save the world? She was only in fourth grade, for goodness' sake.

But the more she thought about it, the more she couldn't get it out of her head. For some reason, saving the world sounded good to her.

There was only one thing to do. She snatched the cape from the box and ran out into the backyard. She knew she wasn't ready to save the world. Not yet. Not before talking it over with Grandpa Joe.

2

Sheriff Joe

Jo didn't exactly know how to bring up the subject of saving the world. But her grandpa Joe had been a sheriff for thirty-five years. If anyone would have an opinion on the matter of doing battle with evil villains, he would. He might not know anything about stopping trains and flying, but you have to start somewhere.

Jo knocked on the door of her grandfather's shack.

"Who's there?" came a voice.

"It's Jo."

"Joe?"

"No, Jo."

"Oh, *Jo*. I thought I was talking to myself for a second there. Come in, Jo."

Jo went inside. On the walls she saw pictures of her grandfather catching bad guys, shaking hands with the mayor, receiving awards for bravery. Thirty-five years' worth of police work. The walls were covered with it.

"Did you like catching bad guys, Gramps?" Jo asked.

"What's that? You have bad eyes and cramps? Here, try my spectacles."

Her grandpa didn't hear very well. Jo raised her voice and tried again. "I said, 'Did you like catching bad guys?'"

"Like it? I wish I was out there right now."

"But was it fun?" Jo was big on having fun. If

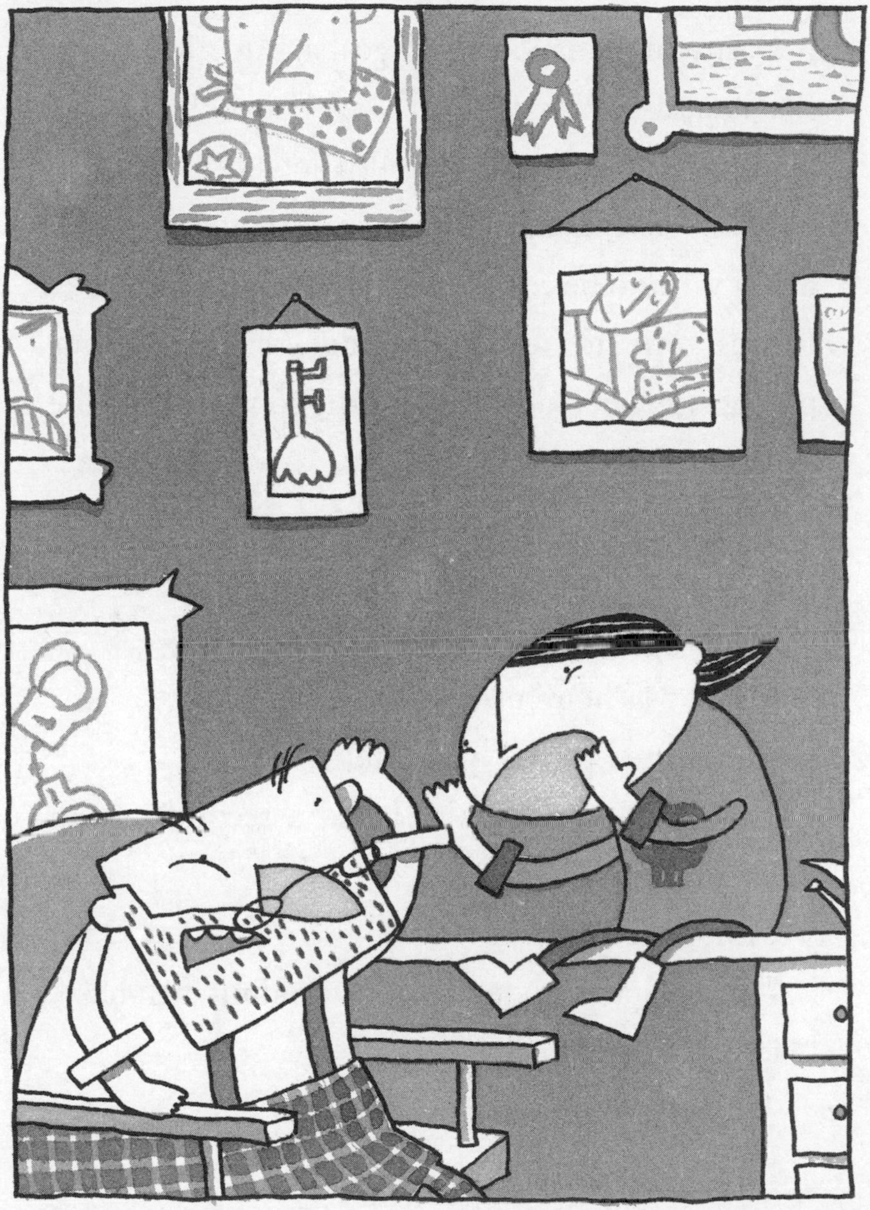

it wasn't fun, maybe she'd go back to riding her skateboard—and gazing at David's freckles.

"I had a blast," said Grandpa Joe.

This was exactly what Jo wanted to hear. She didn't want to be a superhero if it wasn't enjoyable. It was time to tell him about the mysterious package, she decided. It was time to show him the cape.

"You have an uncle George?" he asked.

"He was my mom's second cousin once removed."

"Why was he removed?"

"They used to call him Stinky George."

Grandpa Joe nodded. "I had a second cousin *twice* removed."

"You mean—?"

"Yes," Grandpa Joe said, wrinkling his nose. "He was a two-time offender."

"Shall I try on the cape?" Jo asked.

"Absolutely."

Jo gave the cape a sniff, just in case it still smelled like Stinky George. Then she draped it over her shoulders and tied it around her neck. "How do I look, Gramps?"

"Like you're ready to save the world," he said.

3

Is There a Sidekick in the House?

Actually, the cape was a bit long for a fourth-grader. But that was fixable—it could be trimmed. Jo was just thankful that her new uniform didn't involve wearing tights. She wouldn't be caught dead wearing tights. She wouldn't even be caught alive in them.

"First things first," Grandpa Joe said. "We trim your cape to fit." He grabbed a pair of scissors and trimmed away. He was one excited grandpa. He'd been wanting to get back into police work for years. And superhero work was kind of like police work, wasn't it? It just had a little more pizzazz. To be honest, it had a lot more pizzazz. Yes, a granddaughter superhero sounded very good to Grandpa Joe.

He trimmed the cape so that it hung almost to Jo's ankles, long enough to make her look like a superhero, but not so long that she'd trip over it.

He tossed the extra material aside. It landed on top of Jo's dog, Raymond.

"Hmm . . ." Jo said. She was surprised at how good Raymond looked with the cape draped over him. Every superhero needed a sidekick, right? "Hmm . . ." she said again. "What if—"

She bent down and tied the cape around Raymond's neck. It was a perfect fit. But something came over Raymond. He started drooling way more than usual. Way, *way* more than usual.

"Get him out of here before we drown!" yelled Grandpa Joe.

Jo sent the drooling Raymond outside, where he began chasing his tail. Chasing his tail was one of Raymond's favorite hobbies, second only to chasing mailmen. But this time he chased his tail at such superhero speed that he drilled a hole right into the backyard.

"Nice," Grandpa Joe said. "I've always wanted a Jacuzzi. Get the hose, Jo."

Jo grabbed the hose and looked at her dog with admiration. Jo Schmo, Superhero, now had a sidekick. A slobbery one, but he would have to do.

4

The Mad Scientist's Lair

You may be asking yourself, "Why are scientists always mad? Why aren't they happy—or at least mildly amused?" Who knows? It may be from years of sniffing strange chemicals in test tubes. It does something to the human brain, and before you know it, you have a mad scientist on your hands.

This was not the case with Dr. Dastardly. He was mad almost from the beginning. One day he'd stubbed his toe on a table leg, and he'd been

mad ever since. Add to this many years of sniffing strange chemicals in test tubes, and you had one scary mad scientist.

Dr. Dastardly was up to no good because of his toe . . . and his brain. While Jo Schmo was filling a hole with water in her backyard, a hole created by the tail-chasing Raymond, Dr. Dastardly put his head back and laughed his evil laugh: *"Mwah-ha-ha!"*

A few seconds later, his assistant, Pete, showed up. "You rang, Dr. Dastardly?"

Dr. Dastardly didn't ring a bell when he needed help . . . he laughed his evil laugh. "Yes, I rang." (Actually, he had laughed.) Dr. Dastardly pointed across the room. "My latest creation, Pete. The Re-animator Laminator! *Mwah-ha-ha!*"

"You rang, Dr. Dastardly?"

"No, I didn't ring. Don't you know an evil laugh when you hear one?"

Pete didn't know the difference. Neither did anyone else. Dr. Dastardly had one way of laughing. Sometimes it meant he needed Pete; sometimes it was an expression of joy. It was all very confusing—especially to Pete.

Dr. Dastardly had been working on the Re-animator Laminator for years. Now it was time to try it out. He picked up the device, which looked like an oversize ray gun, and aimed it across the room at a human skeleton hanging on a hook.

Zap! Immediately the skeleton came to life, and it would have started walking around if it hadn't

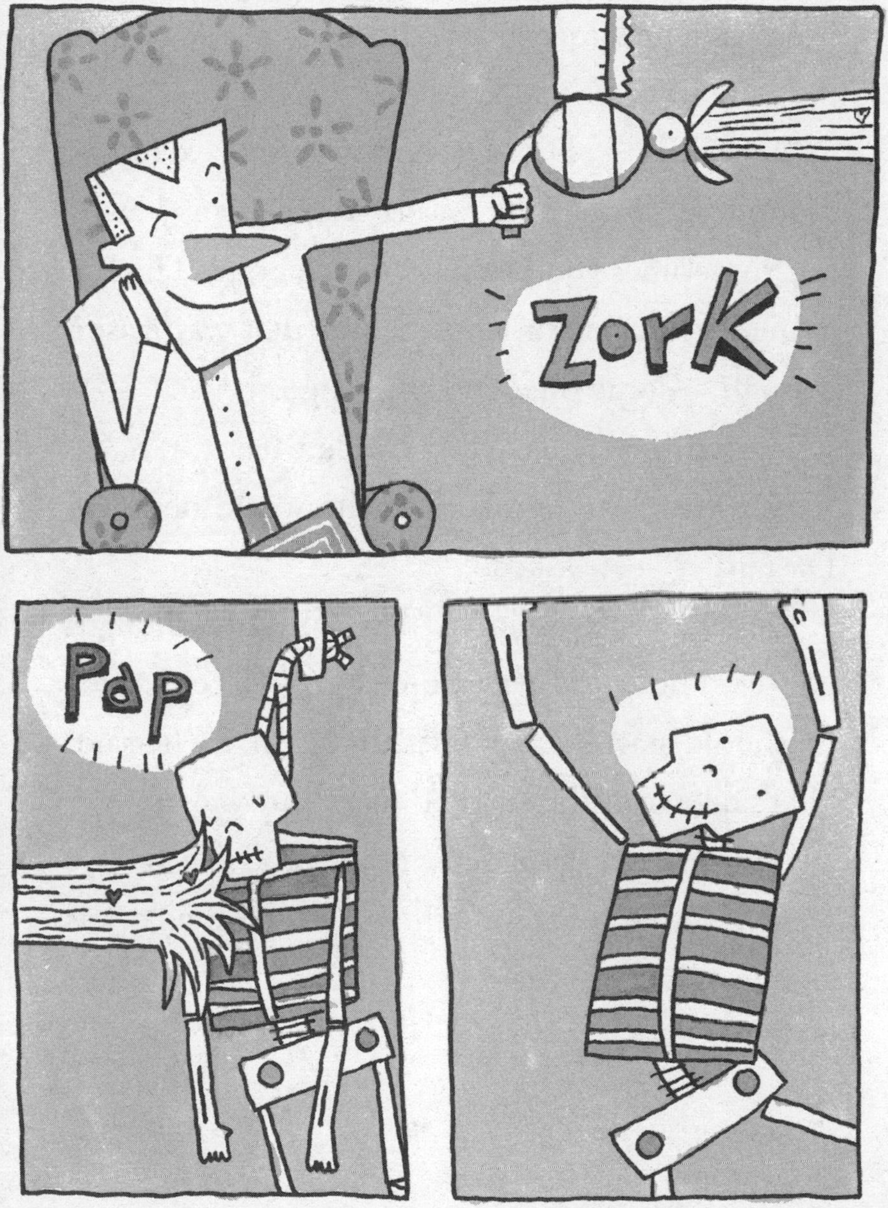
ZorK
PaP

been attached to a hook. Instead it hung there flapping its arms and legs.

"It works!" Dr. Dastardly began dancing around the room. He wasn't much of a dancer, but sometimes you just have to celebrate. The Re-animator Laminator worked, and that was reason enough. "Come on, Pete, let's tango."

It wasn't pretty. Pete had two left feet.

"Are we going to take over the world now, Dr. Dastardly?" Pete asked.

Dr. Dastardly scratched his chin and thought it over. The world was a pretty big place. Maybe he should start small. "First things first," he said. "Let's take over the city and work our way up."

"Sounds like a plan," said Pete. He'd always wanted to take over something. San Francisco was a good place to start.

5

Meanwhile, Back at the Jacuzzi

The cape from Uncle George came with a set of instructions. Jo found them in the mysterious package. "Where do we start?" she asked Grandpa Joe.

"Don't all superheroes fly?"

"I don't know. Do they?"

"Beats me, but flying sounds like fun." Grandpa Joe pointed to the *Superhero Instruction Manual*. "See what it says about flying."

Jo flipped through the pages until she found the

section on flying. She read it out loud: "'Flying is all about thinking properly. Think lofty thoughts and you'll be up in the air in no time.'" She paused. "Hmm . . ."

"Hmm . . . is right," Grandpa Joe agreed. "Unusual instruction manual."

Lofty thoughts? Jo wondered as she walked back and forth in front of the hole created by Raymond. *Lofty thoughts.* Just then a butterfly flitted past. Butterflies are lofty.

Jo spread her arms out and concentrated. *Butterfly,* she thought. Nothing happened. She tried harder. *Butterfly, butterfly, butterfly.* She stayed on the ground.

She looked up and saw puffy clouds floating by. Clouds were lofty. *Clouds, clouds, clouds.* But that didn't work either.

Maybe she needed to jump while thinking lofty thoughts. She climbed on top of the railing of the back porch and launched herself, thinking of both butterflies and clouds at the same time. *Whap!* Then she tried it again, thinking of butterflies *made of* clouds. Jo hit the ground just as hard as before.

"Are you sure you're thinking lofty enough?" Grandpa Joe asked.

"I'm trying to, Gramps."

"Well, try harder."

Lofty thoughts? Jo wondered as she paced. "I got it!" She climbed onto the porch. "Truth!" she yelled as she launched herself . . . and crashed. She got up and tried again. "Liberty!" she called out . . . and hit the ground. Then, "All people are created equal!" which was the loftiest thought she could come up with. But the result was the same. She couldn't get up in the air no matter how hard she tried, or how lofty her ideas.

"Let's try something else," suggested Grandpa Joe, looking through the manual. "Here's a chapter on stopping trains. Want to give it a try?"

Jo dusted herself off. "Sure," she said. But she was starting to lose confidence. Confidence in herself and confidence in Uncle George and his mysterious package.

"It says here that stopping a train is all in the wrist." Grandpa Joe decided that he'd be the reader and Jo would be the doer. After all, he was retired.

And standing on train tracks waiting to get run over sounded kind of scary. Plus, it might hurt!

Jo, on the other hand, had a red cape. She looked very superhero-ish. Maybe she could pull it off. She stood on the tracks as a train raced toward her. "All in the wrist? Are you kidding me?"

"That's what it says," Grandpa Joe said. He showed her the diagram. "Here comes the train. Get ready."

Gulp! Jo swallowed hard. She moved her wrists just so. She even threw in a few lofty thoughts. The train blew its whistle and it rushed at her. And—

Before you could say "Jo Schmo stopped the train," Jo Schmo stopped the train. Just like that. It really was all in the wrist.

"Wow!" Jo said. "Did you see that, Gramps? I just stopped a train!"

Grandpa Joe jumped up and down. Well, he jumped as well as an old man with a cane could. "You did it, Jo! You stopped a train!"

Jo rotated her wrists a few times. "Wow," she said again. "It really is all in the wrist."

The train, of course, was completely demolished, but at least Jo Schmo wasn't.

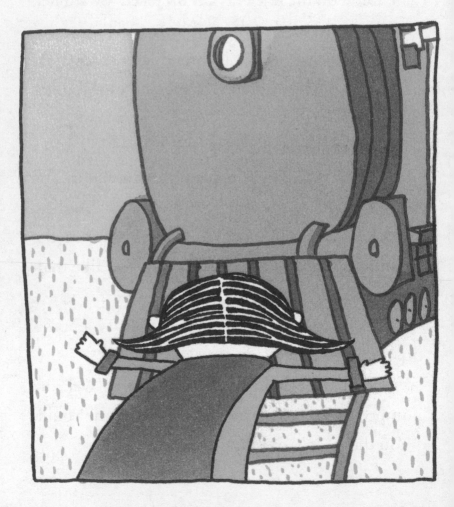

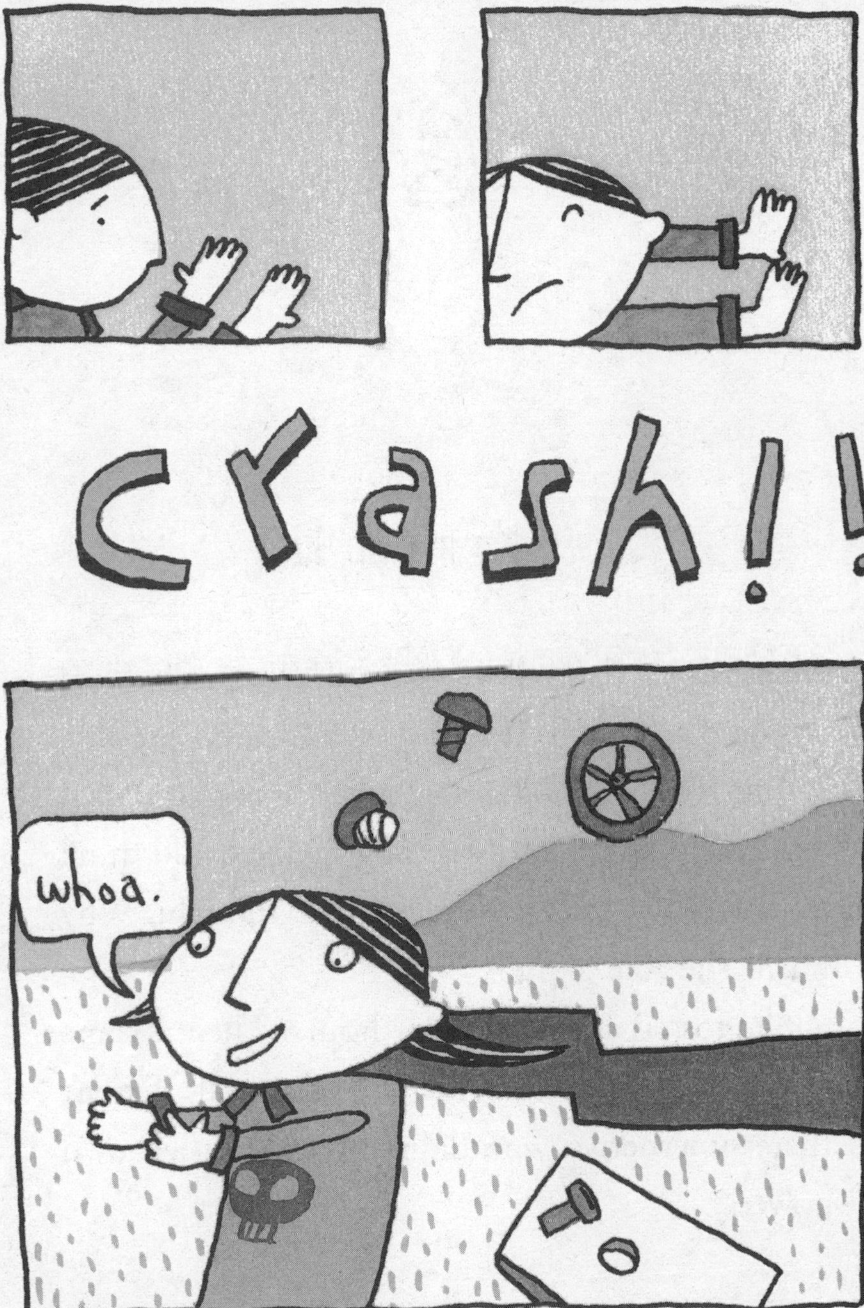
crash!!
whoa.

6

Jo Schmo Has an Idea

That night Jo couldn't get to sleep. She had absolutely adored stopping that train, but she couldn't stop thinking about her flying attempts. She had used the loftiest thoughts she could think of, maybe the loftiest thoughts ever thought. Why wasn't she able to fly?

She tossed and turned for hours. Then it came to her. Maybe she didn't have to fly at all. Weren't there superheroes who didn't fly under their own power?

28

She jumped out of bed and turned on the light. Her dog, Raymond, opened one eye and looked at her with an expression that said, "This better be important."

Jo ignored him and pulled a book from her shelf, the *Encyclopedia of Superheroes.* She flipped through the pages. "Aha!" she said to Raymond, who was still looking at her with one eye. "Not all superheroes can fly under their own power."

Raymond's expression said, "Ask me if I care."

"Wonder Woman flew an invisible plane. And look at Batman—he couldn't fly. But he did have a great car, didn't he? A very great car." Jo put down the book. Maybe she didn't have to fly. Maybe she just needed a terrific vehicle.

Hmm . . . she thought. There was no way she could drive a car. She was only in fourth grade, for goodness' sake. But what about her motorized skateboard? Her skateboard could be her . . . Schmomobile.

Yes, her skateboard was the key, she decided. It just needed a little more power. Actually, it needed a lot more. If she was going to catch bad guys and save the world, then her skateboard needed a lot more power.

"Come on, Raymond," she whispered as she tiptoed down the hall.

Raymond's look said, "Do I have to?"

He went anyway. He had a reputation as man's best friend, and he wanted to keep it that way.

Jo got to work that very night whipping her skateboard into superhero shape. There was a broken-down car that had been in her garage

for years. "Spare parts galore," she whispered to Raymond.

She worked all night, using parts from the old car, and in the morning her superpowered Schmomobile was complete. Turbocharged and everything. Zero to sixty in 4.3 seconds. Actually, she wasn't sure how fast it would go. But it sure looked fast.

Even Raymond thought so.

Dr. Dastardly's Evil Plan

"Mwah-ha-ha!"

"You rang, Dr. Dastardly?"

"Yes, Pete, I'd like a cup of tea with a slice of lemon. Shaken, not stirred."

"You got it." Pete returned a moment later with just what the doctor ordered.

Dr. Dastardly took a small sip, then put the cup aside. "Now to begin my evil plan." He tossed his head back and laughed his evil laugh. *"Mwah-ha-ha!"*

"You rang?"

"No, Pete. That was just an evil laugh."

"Oh, right."

Dr. Dastardly picked up the Re-animator Laminator and zapped the skeleton one more time, just to make sure it really did work. Just like before, the skeleton began flapping its arms and legs.

"It works!" Dr. Dastardly yelled all over again. He glanced at Pete. "I don't suppose you want to tango?"

Pete looked down at his two left feet. "I'd rather not."

"Right. Back to our evil plan. With the Re-animator Laminator I can take over the city, and then . . . the world." He looked at his assistant. "What are the scariest creatures ever to walk the Earth, Pete?"

"Uh . . . mothers-in-law."

"Oh, right," Dr. Dastardly said. "What are the

second-scariest creatures?" When Pete didn't reply, the doctor answered for him. "Dinosaurs."

"Dinosaurs are extinct." Pete never graduated from high school, but even he knew that.

"That's where the Re-animator Laminator comes in." Dr. Dastardly was so excited that he threw his head back and—*"Mwah-ha-ha!"*

"Evil laugh?" Pete asked.

"Yes," the doctor said, "but can I have a refill of my tea?"

8

The Schmomobile

Jo Schmo couldn't fly, but neither could Batman, and that was good enough for Jo. And, like Batman, Jo now had a cool vehicle to make up for her lack of flying. The next day she took the Schmomobile out for a spin before school. Just as she thought, it did zero to sixty in 4.3 seconds. Grandpa Joe stood on the sidewalk with a stopwatch to make sure.

"Yep," he said, giving the watch a click, "four point three. That is one impressive skateboard."

Jo thought so too. And she was pretty sure Batman would approve.

"Off to school with you, Jo," Grandpa Joe said. "I'll text you if I hear anything."

That was the plan. Grandpa Joe had given Jo a cell phone. He'd sit in his shack, listening to the police radio. If a serious crime occurred, he'd send his granddaughter a text message. The rest was up to her.

Jo sped away on the Schmomobile, waving goodbye to Gramps.

The Schmomobile was the biggest thing to hit Prairie Street Elementary School since summer vacations. While the girls gathered around, admiring her cape, the boys admired Jo's new mode of transportation.

Kevin, Mitch, and David thought it was the coolest thing since the Batmobile. So did Tom, Dick, and Harry.

When the bell rang, no one wanted to go inside.

"I want a cape just like yours," said Kim.

"I want a skateboard just like yours," said Kevin.

"Let's go inside," said Jo. She didn't mind being popular for once in her life, but school was starting. Being popular would have to wait.

It was a school day just like any other. At least it was at first. Megan led the pledge. Jill gave her oral report on the invention of ice cream. The rest of the day was work, work, work.

And then, right in the middle of a math word problem involving leftover lunch money and how many Popsicles Charlie could purchase with one dollar and twenty-three cents, Jo got a text message from her grandfather.

Bank robbery on Market Street.
Our first mission. Go get 'em, Jo.

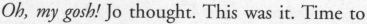

Oh, my gosh! Jo thought. This was it. Time to  see if she could do what superheroes do. Stopping a train was one thing, but catching real bad guys? Could she handle that?

While Jo Schmo was thinking it over, David turned around in his chair and looked her in the eye. David with his seventeen freckles she absolutely adored.

"Can I borrow a pencil, Jo?" he asked.

Oh, no! This was a distraction she didn't need. Bank robbers were committing crimes and needed to be caught. Jo tore her eyes away from David.

Unfortunately, they landed on Mitch. And he was wearing green. Mitch looked spectacular in green. She had to get out of there—and quick.

She raised her hand. "Mrs. Freep, can I go to the bathroom?"

On her way out the door, Jo came face to face with Kevin and his great head of hair. Oh, no! Not again. David, Mitch, and Kevin—that is what you call a triple whammy. Superman had Kryptonite;

Jo Schmo had David, Mitch, and Kevin.

She shoved herself out of the classroom just in time before she fainted. Then she tore across the playground to the bike rack and the Schmomobile.

9

Simon and Ralph

Simon and Ralph were bank robbers, and they were pretty good at it. After all, they'd both graduated from the Bank Robber School of America. They may have graduated at the bottom of their class, but still, they graduated. How many bad guys do you know who have degrees in bank robbery?

Simon and Ralph were a team. Ralph was the safecracker and driver of the getaway vehicle. Simon was the master of disguise. Actually, he wasn't really a master. Although he'd taken several classes on the subject, he'd gotten Ds in all of them.

Simon wasn't the sharpest knife in the drawer. Neither was Ralph.

Maybe this was why they were partners.

And so on the day of the Market Street bank robbery, Simon looked at Ralph and said, "I'll disguise myself as you, and you disguise yourself as me."

There was something very wrong with this idea, Ralph thought. But he went along with it. He didn't know any better, since he'd taken the same disguise classes and gotten the same grades.

Yes, these two were made for each other.

They burst into a bank on Market Street, dressed as each other, and yelled the words they were taught to yell in bank robbers' school. "Stick 'em up!"

The workers and customers of the bank did

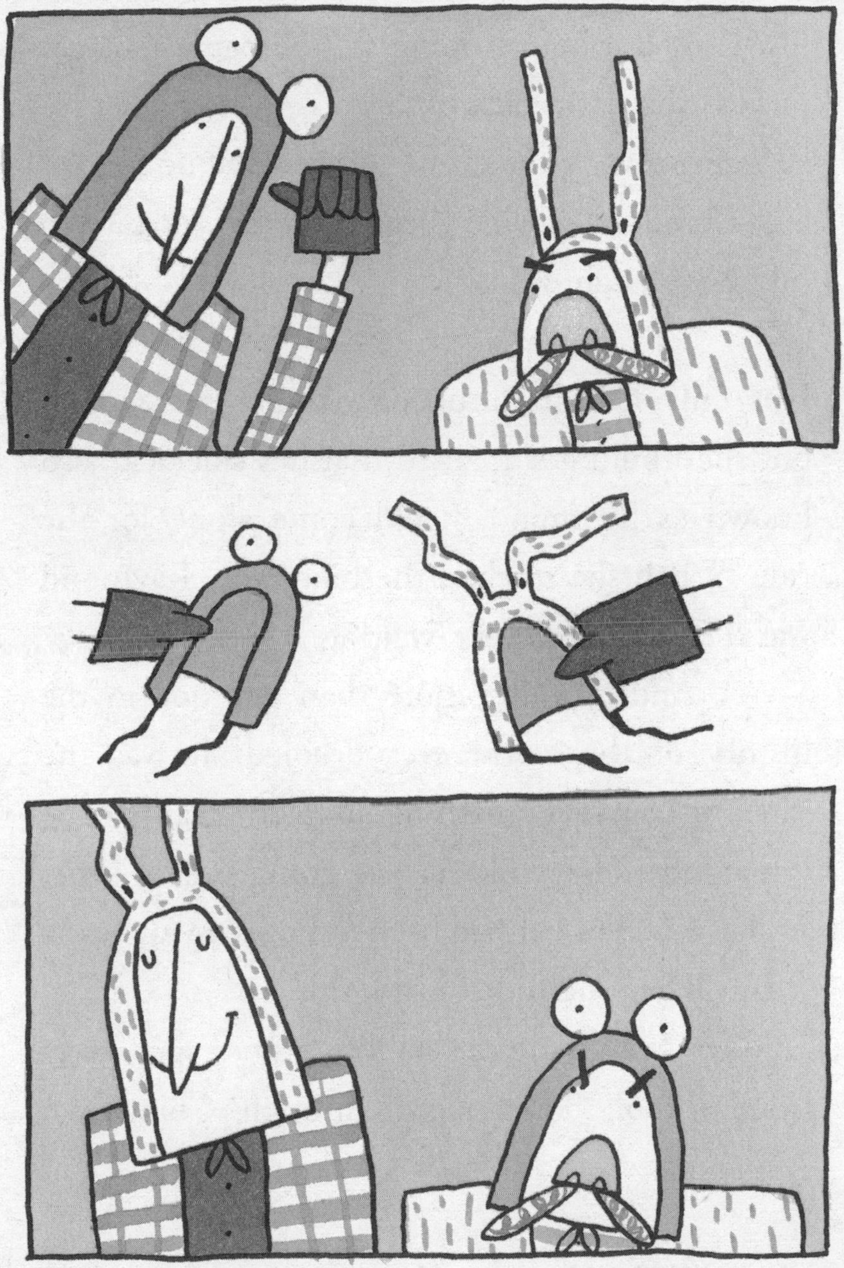

just that. But before doing so, the bank manager pushed the alarm button.

Soon news of the crime reached the police . . . and Grandpa Joe, who then sent a text message to his granddaughter Jo.

Not only had Jo turbocharged her skateboard, but she'd built a sidecar so that her sidekick, also known as Raymond, could come along for the ride. When she reached the bike rack, Raymond was there in the sidecar, waiting.

. . . And drooling more than any dog in the history of the world ever drooled. It was the cape, of course. Something about the cape made Raymond slobber like it was going out of style. And it was. Slobber had been out of style for years.

But Raymond didn't know this.

Jo tried to ignore the slobber as they sped away from school. They raced through Chinatown toward Market Street, hitting sixty miles an hour in 4.3 seconds just as before.

Sixty miles an hour is pretty fast on a city street. It's even faster on a sidewalk. The Schmomobile weaved and dodged through the crowds of Chinatown, then did the same on Market Street.

Raymond stopped drooling long enough to look at Jo with an expression that said, "I do believe we're getting close."

"Dead ahead!" yelled Jo.

She skidded to a stop in front of the bank just as Simon, who was dressed up as Ralph, and Ralph, who was dressed up as Simon, were climbing into their getaway vehicle.

"Halt in the name of—" Jo began.

Halt in the name of what? she thought. What kind of lofty thought should she throw in there after "Halt in the name of"? Halt in the name of a superhero and her dog? Halt in the name of truth,

justice, and the American way? Halt in the name
of ice cream? Halt in the name of—

While she was in the middle of pondering which
lofty thought to add after "Halt in the name of,"
Raymond tugged on her cape and looked at her
with an expression that said, "Can we hurry this
up? The bad guys are getting away."

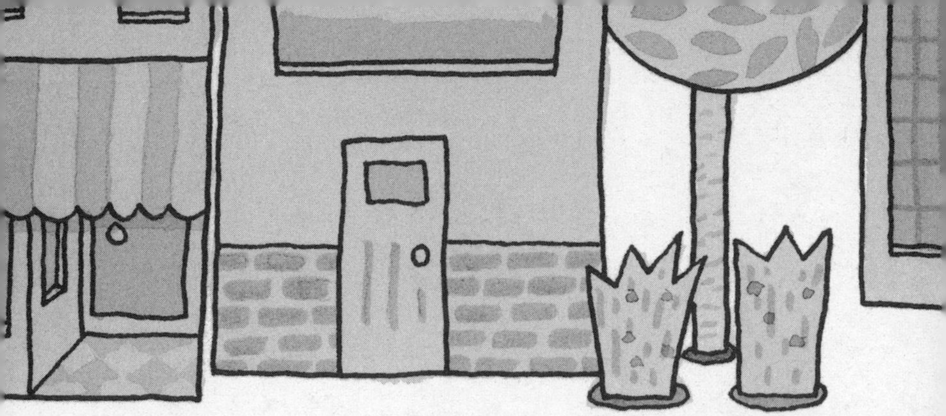

Actually, the bad guys had gotten away—they had completely vanished from Market Street.

"Halt because I said so!" yelled Jo finally.

But it was too late. Simon and Ralph were nowhere to be seen.

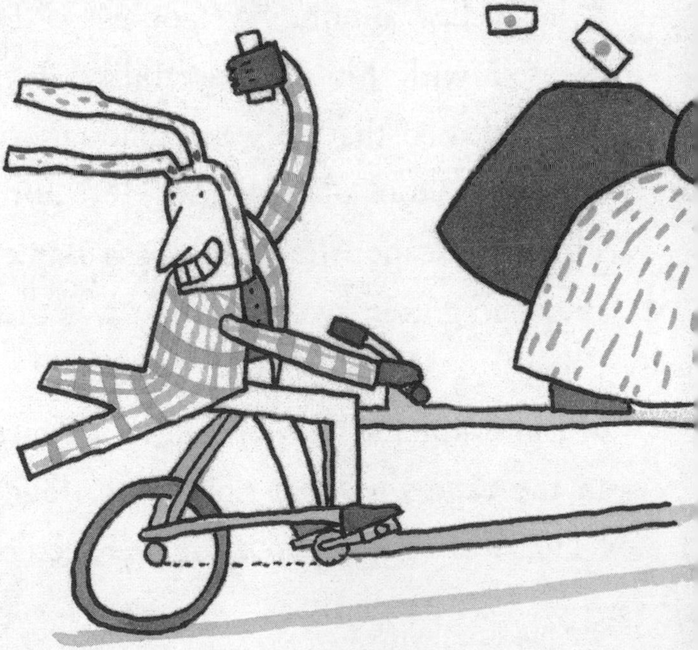

10

The Abandoned Warehouse District

"Ha!" yelled Simon. "We got away." He was very pleased with his driving ability. He was even more pleased that he was a graduate of the Bank Robber School of America. He'd gotten a D in How to Escape After Robbing a Bank class. Still, they had gotten away, and that was the important thing.

But Ralph looked worried. "Did you see that girl in the cape with that slobbering dog?" he asked. "That was a superhero if I've ever seen one." Ralph had never seen one. What did he know? She may have been just a girl in a cape with a dog who was dreaming of cheeseburgers.

"You worry too much, Ralph." Simon gestured to the buildings around them. "We're in the abandoned warehouse district. We're safe. Even if she is a superhero, she'll never find us."

Simon had a point. Businesses were failing left and right in the city, which meant the abandoned warehouse district was growing. There were lots of places to hide, especially for two graduates of bank robbing school.

Still, Ralph didn't feel right. He went to the door and peeked outside.

The bank robbers had vanished, but Jo Schmo wasn't giving up. This was her first mission. Her grandfather was counting on her. So was every law-abiding citizen in San Francisco. Jo couldn't let them down.

She kicked her supercharged skateboard into high gear and sped down Market Street.

The bad guys had gotten away, but not for long, if she had anything to say about it. She glanced down at Raymond, who was busy slobbering—and he wasn't thinking of cheeseburgers. "Any ideas, Raymond?"

Raymond gave her a look that said, "To the abandoned warehouse district, and make it snappy!" Raymond may have been a dog, but even he knew where villains liked to hide.

"The warehouse district it is," said Jo.

In no time at all, they were cruising the streets of the district. And it was no small area. Hundreds of bad guys lived here. And only two of them were guilty of robbing the bank on Market Street.

Where to start? Jo looked around, hoping something would catch her eye. Something suspicious, like two guys walking along holding sacks of money, or maybe someone with an evil laugh. An evil laugh was a dead giveaway. If you were laughing evilly, it usually meant that you had been successful in committing some sort of crime, like robbing a bank.

Jo listened carefully. Nope, no evil laughs. Not even any non-evil ones. It was just—

And that's when she saw it: a pair of eyes looking at her through a crack in a door. Those were a bank robber's eyes or she wasn't Jo Schmo. And she was definitely Jo Schmo. She looked at her dog. "What's my name, Raymond?"

"Jo Schmo," said Raymond's look.

"Just checking."

Jo hit the gas and raced for the set of eyes peering at her through the crack in the door. Zero to sixty in 4.3 seconds.

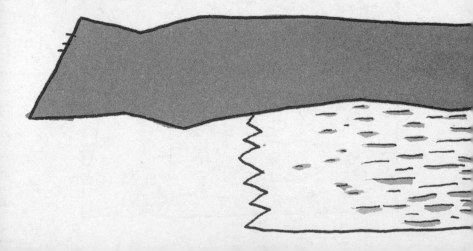

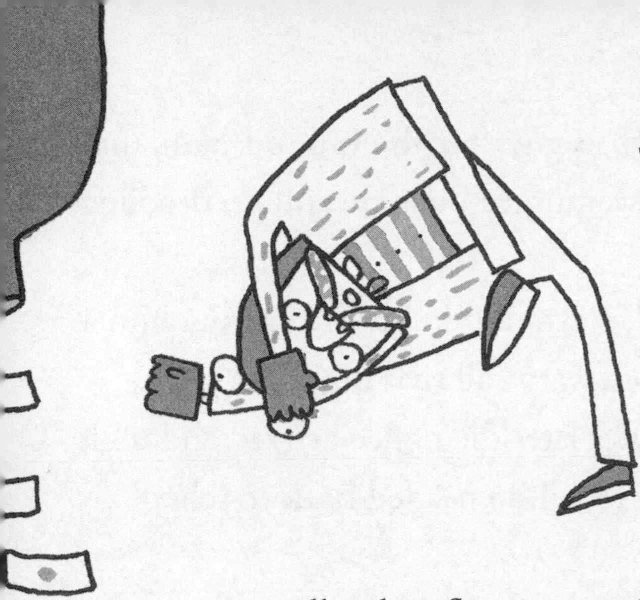

She crashed through the door. Money flew in all directions. So did a couple of bad guys.

Actually, they flew in two directions. Up and then down.

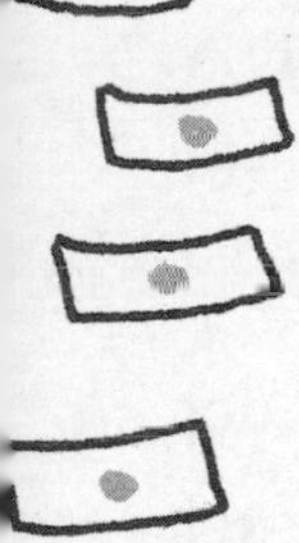

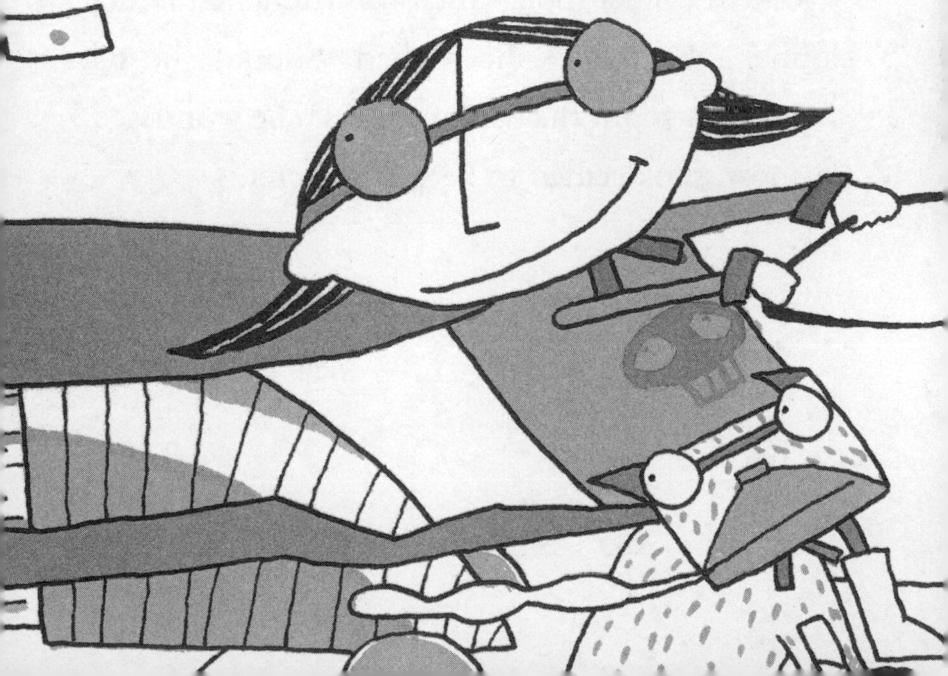

Crash! The bad guys hit the ground hard, and Jo Schmo was waiting for them. Jo and her drooling dog.

"Nice work, Raymond," she said, giving him a high-five, which wasn't all that high.

A few minutes later the police arrived and took the thieves off to jail. Jo headed back to school.

"That was the longest bathroom break in U.S. history," said Mrs. Freep. "What did you do, fall in?"

Jo held up her foot, which was drenched in dog slobber. "Kind of," she replied. Should she tell Mrs. Freep about the bank robbers? she wondered. For now, she decided to keep it a secret.

Every Superhero Needs a Hideout

There were now three water-filled Jacuzzi-size holes in Jo's backyard, created by the tail-chasing Raymond. When she got home after school, Jo's grandfather was sitting in one of them while listening to his police radio.

He climbed out and toweled himself off. "Great work!" he said. "I just heard about it on the radio."

"Thanks, Gramps."

Gramps grabbed his cane and started dancing

around the backyard. His granddaughter had just stopped a couple of villains. It was time to celebrate.

Raymond thought so too. He began chasing his tail again, and before you could say there were four Jacuzzi-size holes in the backyard, there were four Jacuzzi-size holes in the backyard. Just like that.

"Come here, boy," Jo called to her dog. When

he climbed out of the hole and walked over, she removed the cape. There were enough holes in her backyard, and she didn't need any more dog slobber on her shoes.

Grandpa Joe stopped dancing and sat down on the front porch of his little shack. Jo joined him. She grabbed the *Superhero Instruction Manual* and flipped through the pages.

"It says here that all superheroes need some sort of hideout." She scanned the backyard—the holes, the fruit trees, Raymond's doghouse. Then she looked up at Grandpa Joe. "I don't suppose you'd like to donate your shack to the cause?"

"Nothing doing! This is my home."

"No problem," said Jo. "It was just an idea." She looked at the four holes. Maybe she could add a roof to one, she thought. An underground superhero's hideout? She shook her head. Nah, too many worms. Next she considered Raymond's doghouse. It was large enough. It had a roof and a door.

But Raymond was looking at her with an expression that said, "Nothing doing!"

"Hmm . . ." she said to herself. She was a superhero. She had the cape; she had the sidekick; she even had the supercharged vehicle. One thing was missing—a hideout.

"Cheer up, Jo," Gramps said, rubbing her back. "You have a bedroom. It's kind of like a hideout."

Gramps was right. She did have a bedroom, her very own bedroom. It might make the perfect hideout.

Jo jumped to her feet. "Thanks, Gramps," she called as she ran inside. Her bedroom would have to do, but first it needed some sort of sign to make it official. People needed to know that it was no longer just a bedroom. It was headquarters for a very important crime fighter who drove a very cool vehicle.

She dumped her backpack onto the kitchen table and got to work. When she finished, she darted up the stairs and hung the sign on her door.

12

Dr. Dastardly

Dr. Dastardly was drinking his tea and thinking things over. Moments earlier, Pete had brought him the tea with a squeeze of lemon. He'd heard the *Mwah-ha-ha* and figured it wasn't an evil laugh—it was just an evil scientist who was thirsty.

He was right. His boss was thirsty, but he also looked concerned.

"What's up, chief?" Pete asked.

Dr. Dastardly sipped his tea. "What if we bring the dinosaurs to life and we can't control them?

Our plan will fail. We need a dress rehearsal."
Which was kind of strange, because dinosaurs
don't wear clothes.

"Dress rehearsal?" Pete repeated. "But, Dr.
Dastardly, dinosaurs don't wear—"

"I know they don't wear clothes, Pete. We need
to practice, okay?"

"Right."

Dr. Dastardly looked across the room at the
skeleton. "Pete, take the skeleton off the hook. I
want to try something."

When Pete unhooked the skeleton, Dr. Dastardly
pointed the Re-animator Laminator at it.

Zap!

Just like before, the bag of bones came to life.
But this time it wasn't held in place by a hook. It
could move around.

"Skeleton," Dr. Dastardly began, "dance the
tango with Pete."

"But, Dr. Dastardly, I have—"

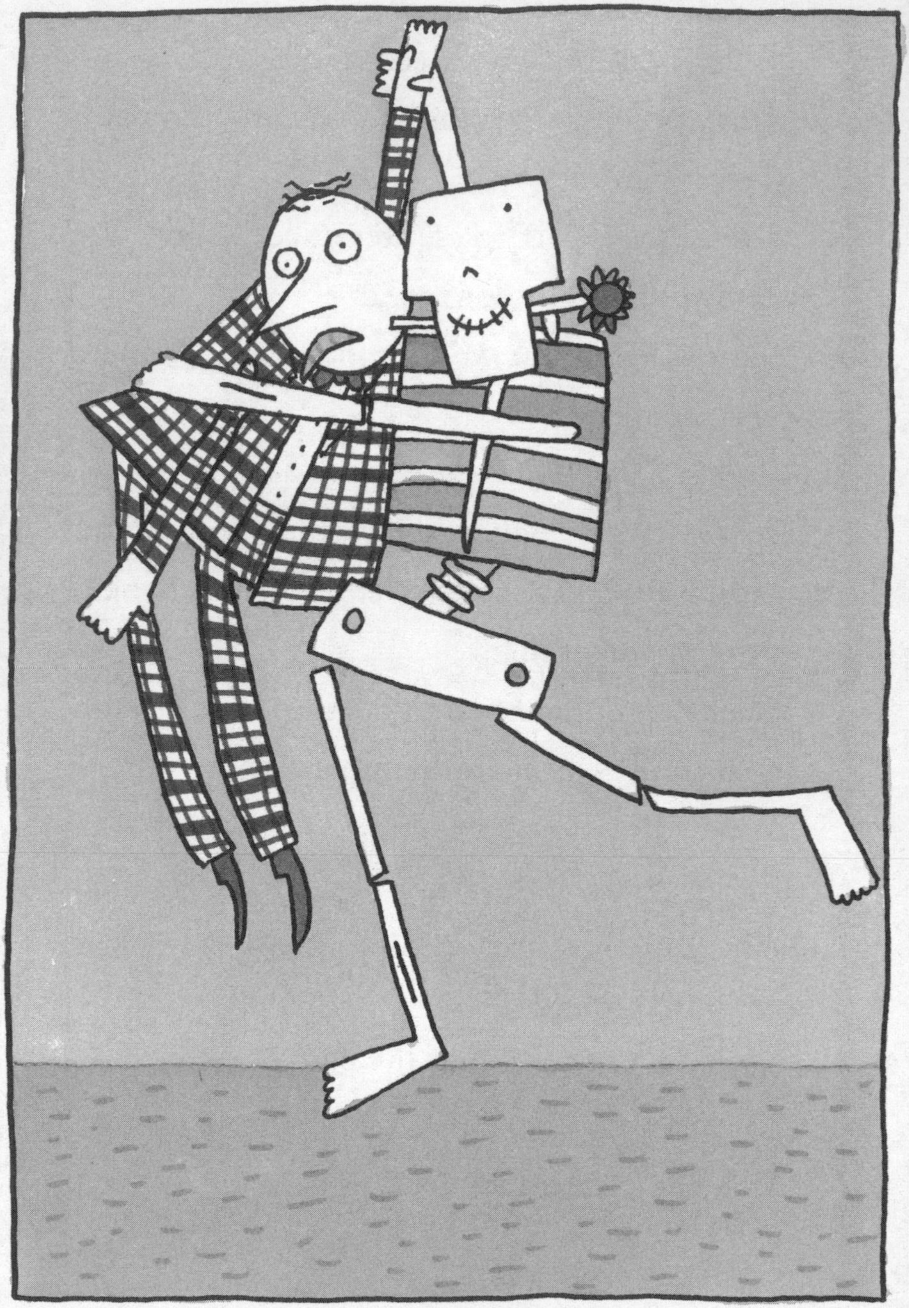

"I know you have two left feet, Pete. Don't worry. The skeleton will lead."

The skeleton did lead. In fact, it had rhythm. Who knew? It danced the tango all over the evil scientist's lair, then went right into the fox trot, followed by the waltz.

Pete was sweating from all the dancing. So was the skeleton!

Dr. Dastardly pressed the button on the Re-animator Laminator, and the skeleton fell to the floor in a heap.

"Mwah-ha-ha!"

"You rang, Dr. Dastardly?"

"No, I didn't ring. The skeleton obeyed instructions. We can control the dinosaurs. We can take over the city."

13

Knuckle Sandwich ... on Rye

It was a busy week for Jo Schmo. She caught drug dealers on Tuesday, nabbed jewel thieves on Wednesday, tackled a few terrorists on Thursday, and rounded out the week on Friday by busting wide open a ring of fortune cookie thieves. All while she was supposed to be in school.

Mrs. Freep, Jo's teacher, was wondering about the long bathroom breaks, and why Jo always returned to class with wet shoes.

The shoes, of course, were the result of Raymond. That dog really knew how to slobber. He could teach a class on the subject.

That evening at dinner, Jo's mom asked, "Why do we have four Jacuzzis in the backyard?"

"Uh . . . *ahem*." Grandpa Joe cleared his throat. "Variety is the spice of life?"

"Yeah, but four?"

"It's Raymond, Mom," Jo said. "When he chases his tail with his cape on, strange things happen."

"Very strange things," said Mrs. Schmo, but she was warming to the idea of four Jacuzzis. Everyone could have his own—even Raymond.

After dinner, Jo and her grandfather went outside in the backyard.

"Show me some crime-fighting tricks, Gramps," Jo said.

"What kind of tricks?" he asked.

"Fighting tricks. Hand-to-hand combat stuff. I'm getting tired of running over the bad guys with the Schmomobile." Although Raymond sure did like it.

"Okay." Her grandfather grabbed her toe and gave it a squeeze.

"Ow, ow, ow!" cried Jo.

"The Russian Toe Hold," Grandpa said proudly.

"Ow," said Jo. She needed that extra "ow." The previous three didn't do the job.

Next he grabbed her ear.

"Ow, ow, ow!" cried Jo.

"The Siberian Ear Tweak," he said as he let go.

"Ow," Jo said, rubbing her ear. "Very effective. Those Russians sure know their stuff."

Grandpa Joe cracked his knuckles. "That's nothing. Wait till you see my best move."

Jo wasn't sure she wanted to. Her toe and ear were still throbbing.

"Put your face over here, Jo."

"My face?" She didn't like the sound of that. "Wouldn't you rather do something with my elbow?"

When Grandpa Joe shook his head, she came closer.

SMACK!

"Ow, ow, ow, ooowwww!"

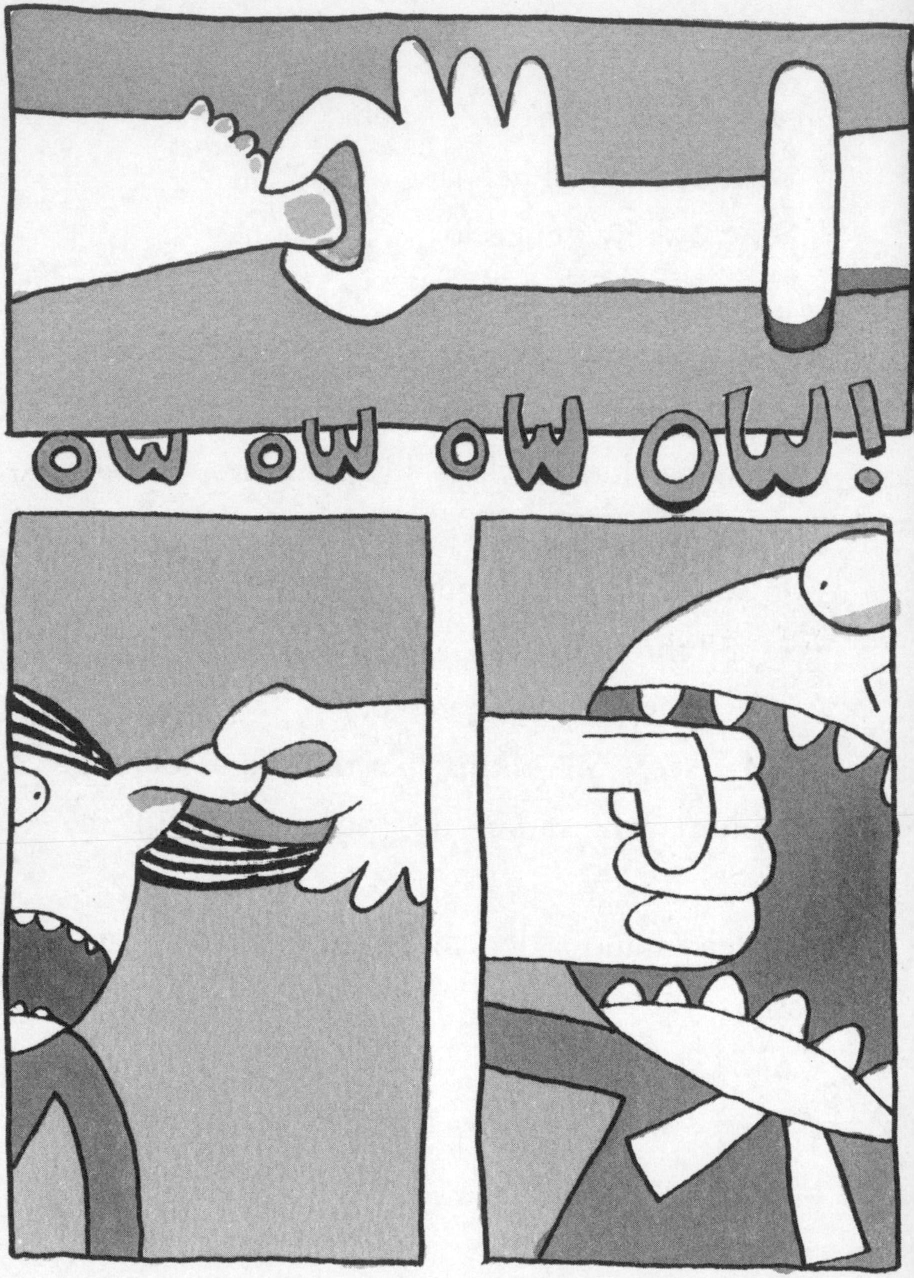
OW OW OW OW!

"The Knuckle Sandwich. My favorite move of all."

It was a good move, all right, Jo thought. It beat the Russian Toe Hold and the Siberian Ear Tweak combined.

"Let me try that one, Gramps," Jo said. "Put your face over here."

SMACK!

"Ow, ow, ow, ooowwww!"

Gramps was right. The Knuckle Sandwich was the best move of all time.

14

MWah-ha-ha!

Jo could hardly wait to try out her new moves on a real bad guy, especially the Knuckle Sandwich. All evening she tried it out on her dog, Raymond, who kept looking at her with an expression that said, "Ow, ow, ow" and "ow."

By bedtime she considered herself an expert.

She went upstairs to her room, but before dropping off to sleep, she tied the end of a piece of string to her big toe. The string led out her window and down to Grandpa Joe's shack. If crimes were

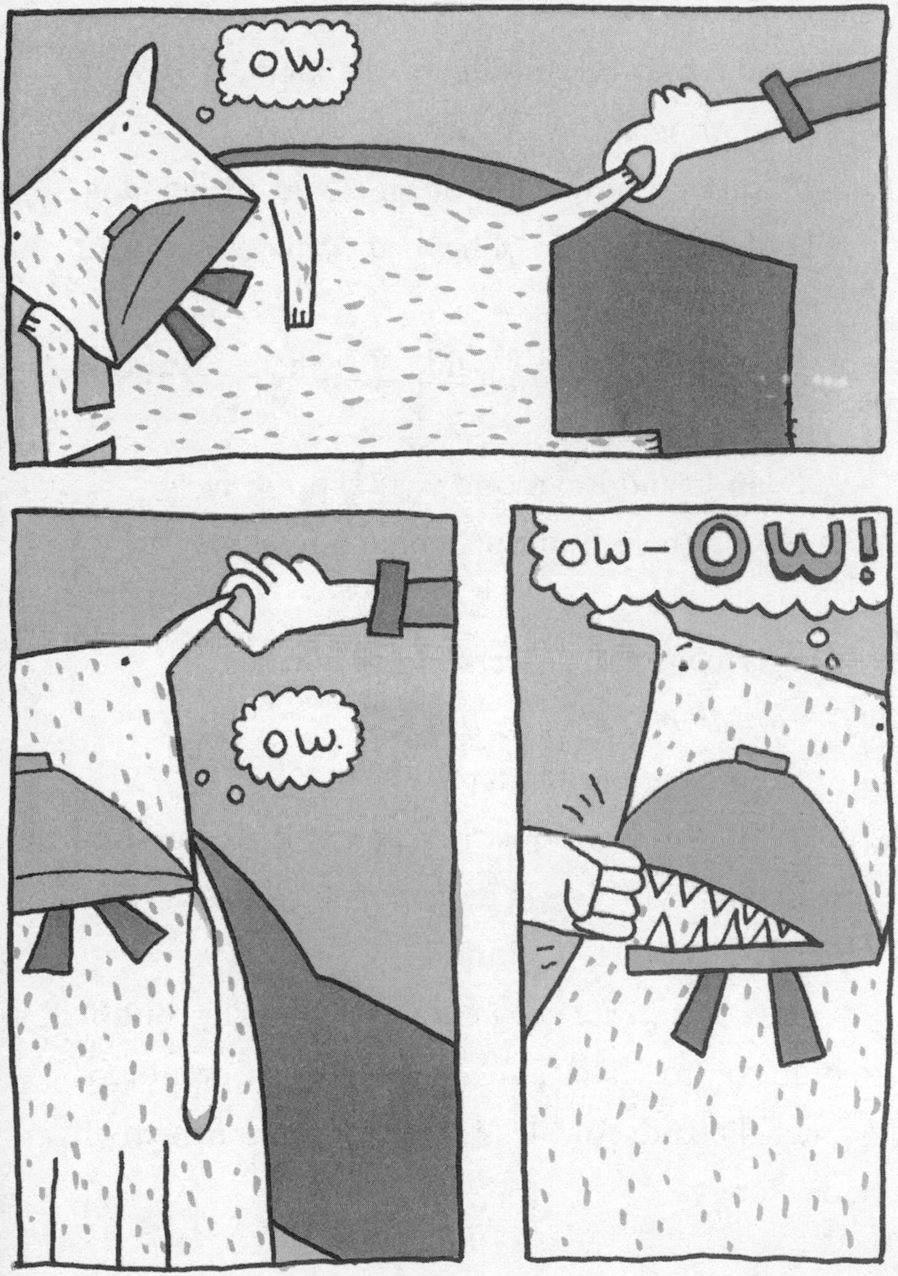
OW.
OW.
OW-OW!

committed in the middle of the night, he'd yank on the string and wake her up.

"Good night, Raymond," Jo said to her dog, who slept at the foot of her bed. "Sorry about your sore jaw."

Raymond's look said, "I hate Knuckle Sandwiches."

Soon Jo and Raymond were snoring away.

So was the rest of the Schmo household.

Across town, things were not so quiet.

"*Mwah-ha-ha.*"

"You rang, Dr. Dastardly?"

"No, Pete, I was just practicing. If all goes well with our evil plan, I'm going to need that evil laugh. How does it sound?"

Like you need a cup of tea, Pete thought. But he didn't say so. "That's an evil laugh if I've ever heard one," he said. And let's face it; he heard them all day long.

"Great," Dr. Dastardly said. "Fire up the van, Pete. Let's go take over the city."

You'd think that a mad scientist like Dr. Dastardly would have a supercharged evil vehicle. Kind of like a dastardly version of Jo Schmo's. This was not the case. It was just a regular van with a sign painted on the side.

Once Pete had the van's engine running, Dr. Dastardly grabbed the Re-animator Laminator and jumped inside. Then he threw his head back. *"Mwah-ha-ha!"*

Pete didn't ask him if he wanted tea. He was pretty sure he didn't.

15

The Re-animator Laminator

"Where to, Dr. Dastardly?"

"The natural history museum, of course."

This made sense. If Dr. Dastardly's evil plan was to re-animate dinosaur bones, there was only one place to go—the natural history museum.

"Doesn't the museum have a night watchman?" Pete asked.

"I have that covered. Drive on, Pete."

Pete drove through the abandoned warehouse district, where just recently bank robbers, jewel thieves, terrorists, and a band of fortune cookie thugs had been captured by a fourth grade superhero. While Dr. Dastardly was practicing his evil laugh and dancing the tango with a skeleton, Pete had been reading up on the local news.

A superhero could be a problem, Pete thought. But he didn't know how much of a problem. Plus, what parent would let a fourth-grader out at night, even if she was a superhero? And so Pete drove on. If Dr. Dastardly could bring dinosaurs to life, he could take care of any problems that came along with it. Like fourth grade girls in capes.

Pete pulled around behind the natural history museum and turned off the engine.

"Other side, Pete," said Dr. Dastardly. "We're going in the front door."

"But what about the night watchman?"

"I told you, I've got that covered."

Pete did as he was told. He was pretty sure that bad guys were supposed to sneak in. Who had ever heard of going in the front door? But what could he say? He was just the sidekick.

Dr. Dastardly jumped out of the van and walked up to the front door of the museum and gave a knock.

Pete wanted to say something. Like, *What the heck are you thinking, Dr. Dastardly? Have you lost your mind? Let's go have some tea and think this over.*

But his boss looked so relaxed that Pete kept quiet. *Maybe he knows something I don't,* thought Pete. This, of course, was true. Dr. Dastardly knew a lot that Pete didn't. He was a doctor, for goodness' sake. Pete hadn't even finished high school.

Dr. Dastardly knocked on the door again. "Watch this, Pete," Dr. Dastardly said with a smile. He switched the Re-animator Laminator to laminator mode. A few seconds later, the night watchman opened the front door, and—

ZAP!

Before you could say "The night watchman was

laminated," the night watchman was laminated. A clear sheet of plastic shot out of the Re-animator Laminator. And, just like that, the night watchman was trapped.

Dr. Dastardly switched the Re-animator Laminator back to animator mode. "Follow me, Pete," he said, feeling an evil laugh coming on. "Let's go bring some dinosaurs to life."

"And take over the city?" Pete asked.

"That too."

16

ZAP!

ZAP! ZAP! ZAP! ZAP! ZAP!

Dr. Dastardly was a busy zapper.

ZAP! ZAP! ZAP! ZAP! ZAAP!

A very busy zapper. He walked through the museum, zapping dinosaurs. Raptors, T. rexes, brontosauruses, gigantic prehistoric birds, and many, many others all came to life with a single zap from the Re-animator Laminator. And all of them were completely under the control of Dr. Dastardly.

Things were going so well that even Pete broke out in an evil laugh.

"Nice one," said Dr. Dastardly.

"Thanks."

The natural history museum was bustling with activity. Dr. Dastardly even animated a couple of trash cans and a drinking fountain, just for the heck of it.

"Follow me," Dr. Dastardly called out as he headed for the front door.

"But, Dr. Dastardly," Pete said, "the dinosaurs can't fit through the door."

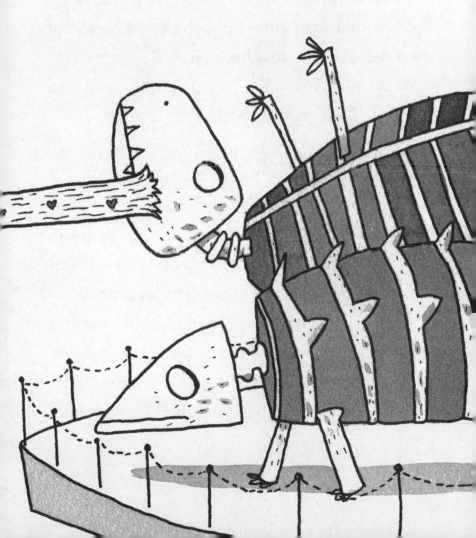

"Not a problem, Pete." He looked up at one of the biggest dinosaurs. "Bronto, make us a new door in that wall."

And before you could say "The brontosaurus broke through the wall and out onto the sidewalk," the brontosaurus broke through the wall and out onto the sidewalk. Just like that.

"*Mwah-ha-ha!*" said Dr. Dastardly and Pete together. Then they high-fived.

Across town, Jo was sound asleep, dreaming of Russian Toe Holds and Knuckle Sandwiches. Now and then she threw in a Siberian Ear Tweak just to break things up. It was a great dream. The villains were losing and she was ahead—by six points!

Until one of the bad guys grabbed her toe and began tugging away. Was this some new version of the Russian Toe Hold? No, it was completely different. And it had a rhythm, like a ringing phone.

Tug, tug, tug. Tug, tug, tug. Yep, exactly like a ringing phone.

Ringing phone!

Jo's eyes flew open. She sat up and looked at her big toe. *Tug, tug, tug.* Grandpa's string! No wonder it seemed like a phone call.

Jo put on her cape, then tied Raymond's around his neck. "Let's go, Raymond." Both of them tore down the stairs and into the backyard, where Grandpa Joe was waiting.

"What is it, Gramps?"

"A dinosaur just ate a Volkswagen on Mason Street."

"A dinosaur?"

"I know, sounds crazy. Better check it out, Jo."

But Jo and Raymond were already racing across the yard to the Schmomobile. She fired up the engine and headed for Mason Street, dog drool trailing behind.

volkswagens, Chevys, and Fords, Oh My!

"Where to, Dr. Dastardly?" Pete asked.

"The mayor's house, of course. We'll take care of the mayor first, and then the city will be ours."

The dinosaurs followed Dr. Dastardly and Pete, snatching up cars and eating them like they were doughnuts as they moved down Mason Street toward the mayor's house.

Pete called out to them, "Don't get too full, now. Leave room for dessert."

The mad scientist shot him a look. "Dessert?"

"The mayor. With a cherry on top and a little salt and pepper."

Dr. Dastardly turned around and addressed the dinosaurs. "Stop eating the cars. We have work to do."

A T. rex that was right in the middle of devouring a school bus dropped it at Dr. Dastardly's feet. He really wanted that school bus—even without a cherry on top or salt

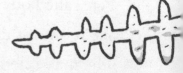

and pepper, it was delicious—but he had to obey.
The Re-animator Laminator made it so.

The other dinosaurs dropped the vehicles they
were eating as well. Dr. Dastardly was in complete
control of them.

"Mwah-ha-ha."

"You rang, Dr. Dastardly?"

"No, I didn't ring, Pete. That was an expression
of joy. Our evil plan
is working."

"Oh."

Halt Because I Said So!

Jo and Raymond raced toward Mason Street. Was it true? she wondered. Was a dinosaur loose in the city, and was it dining on German-made cars?

Nope. It wasn't true. There was way more than one dinosaur loose in the city. And they seemed to like Japanese- and American-made cars just as much. But for now they had stopped eating. They wanted dessert, with or without a cherry on top.

Jo Schmo skidded to a stop in front of Dr.

Dastardly and his team of dinosaurs. "Halt in the name of—"

Once again she needed a lofty thought to go along with "Halt in the name of." But there was no time—any second, she could be trampled by dinosaur feet. As they say, being squashed by a dinosaur can ruin your whole day.

Besides, Raymond was giving her a look that said, "Not again."

"Halt because I said so!" Jo said in her loudest voice.

Only Dr. Dastardly did not stop. Instead he threw his head back

HALT!

and laughed. "*Mwah-ha-ha.* Go home, schoolgirl. It's past your bedtime."

Schoolgirl! Pete thought. Was this the fourth grade superhero who had been catching bad guys right and left in the abandoned warehouse district? "Careful, Dr. Dastardly, she might be trouble."

"Nonsense," said Dr. Dastardly. He glanced over his shoulder at a T. rex and said, "Sic her, boy. And her little dog, too."

The T. rex rushed at Jo, but before you could say "Jo Schmo got him in the Russian Toe Hold and he went down," Jo Schmo got him in the Russian Toe Hold and he went down. Just like that.

And when he did, he shattered.

"*Mwah-ha-ha!*" Jo yelled, then clamped her hand over her mouth.

"Hey," Dr. Dastardly said, "that's my line."

"Not to mention mine," added Pete.

"Sorry," Jo said. "It'll never happen again."

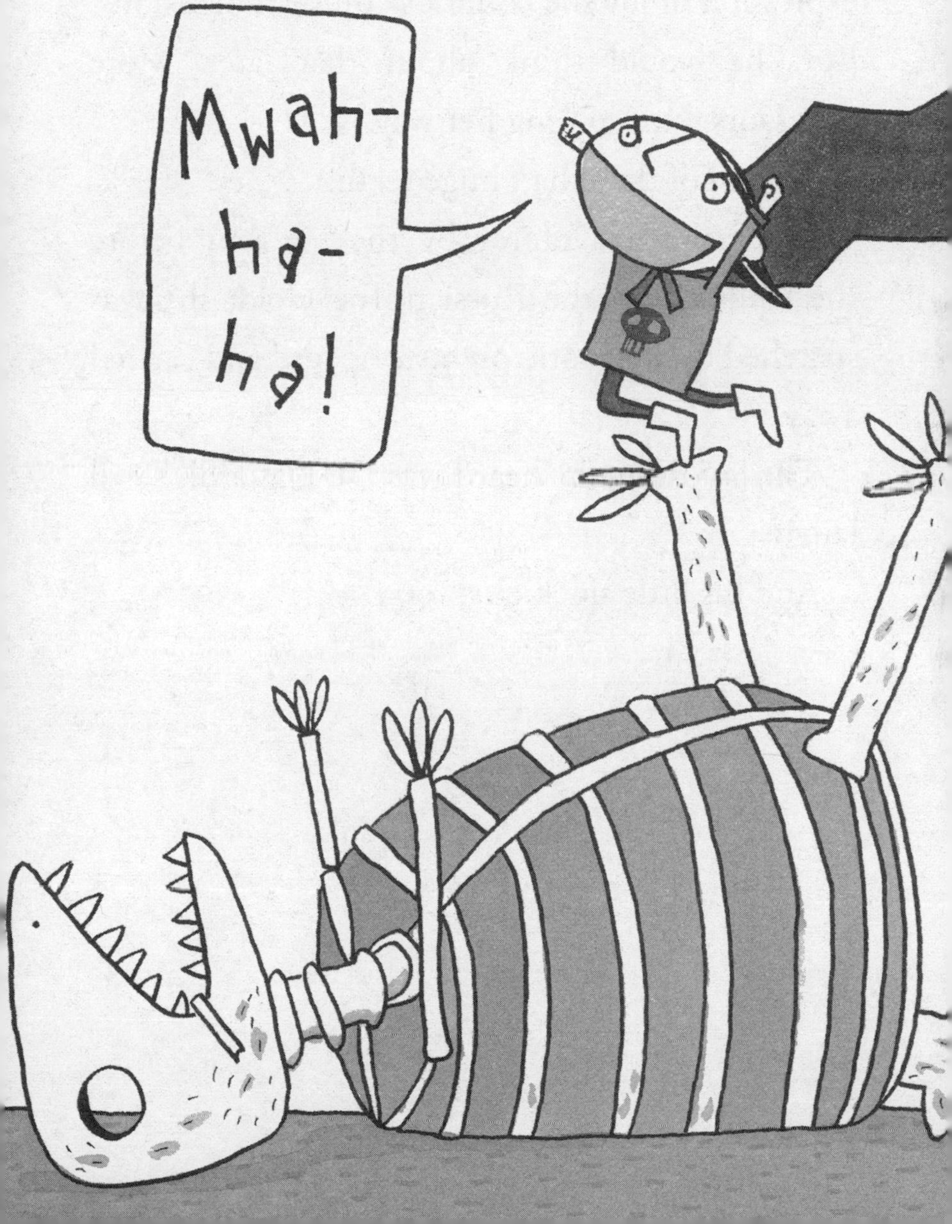
Mwah-ha-ha!

She was just so pleased to have defeated a T. rex, she couldn't help herself. She really needed an expression of joy she could use on such occasions. But she would think about that later. More dinosaurs were coming her way.

And all of them had huge teeth!

She grabbed a raptor by the toe, but before she could apply the Russian Toe Hold, she was snatched by a gigantic prehistoric bird and carried away.

The last thing she heard was Dr. Dastardly's evil laugh.

And his little sidekick's, too.

19

Put Me Down!

"Put me down!" Jo yelled to the prehistoric bird.

Saying this did nothing. Not only was the gigantic bird thinking that Jo might make a better dessert than the mayor, but it didn't even have ears to hear Jo yell "Put me down!" It was just a flying bunch of bones, for goodness' sake.

Jo finally realized this as the bird flew farther and farther away from Mason Street. First she tried the Russian Toe Hold. But which one of the

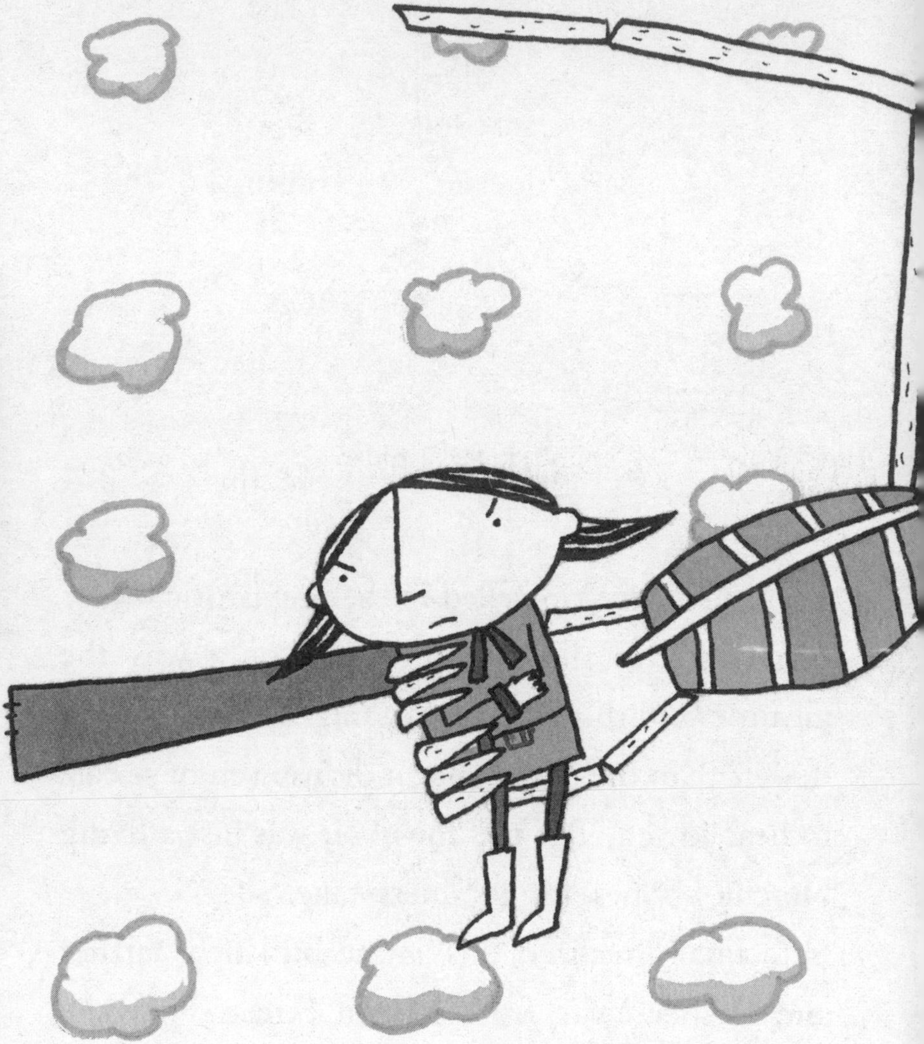

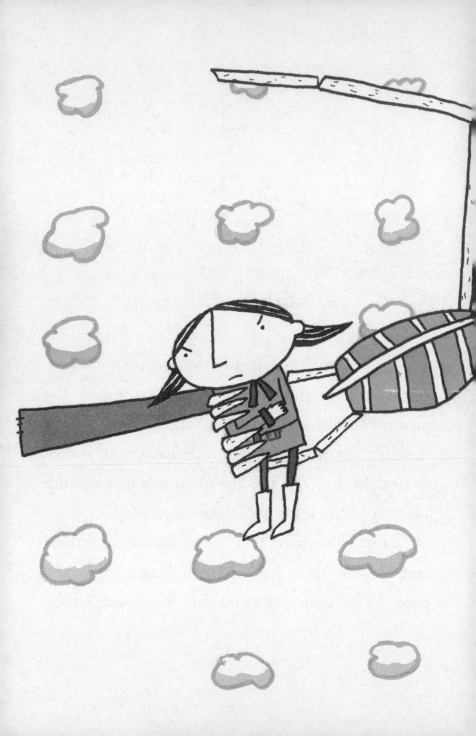

bird's claws was the big toe? Next she considered the Siberian Ear Tweak, which was impossible. There were no ears to tweak.

"Knuckle Sandwich coming right up," Jo said.

SMACK!

The bird shattered just like the T. rex. Jo was free. Unfortunately, she was also hundreds of feet in the air, and she didn't know how to fly.

Down she went.

"Truth," Jo said in desperation. If there was ever a good time for a lofty thought, this was it. "Uh . . . justice. Butterflies. Clouds."

She even flapped her arms. But it was no good.

She landed in a tree and broke every branch on the way down.

"Ouch!"

"Ouch!"

"Ouch!"

"Ouch!"

SPLAT!

Jo dusted herself off and headed back to Mason Street.

20

Jo and Raymond to the Rescue

While Jo Schmo was busy falling from the sky, Raymond was busy running around the ankles of the dinosaurs, barking and slobbering more than any dog in the history of the world had ever slobbered. He would have liked to use the Russian Toe Hold or the Siberian Ear Tweak, but he didn't have hands.

Slobbering would have to do the job.

And it did. Sort of. There was so much dog

slobber on Mason Street that the dinosaurs began to slip and fall.

Jo arrived out of breath and saw what was happening. Of course—dog slobber. Hadn't Gramps said they were in danger of drowning from Raymond's drool?

But they needed more of it—much more.

"Pizza!" yelled Jo, and Raymond drooled even more.

"Hamburgers!"

"Pork chops!"

"Meatballs!"

The more of Raymond's favorite foods Jo called out, the more he drooled. And the more he drooled, the more the dinosaurs slipped and shattered.

But it wasn't enough. Not all of the dinosaurs were falling. They needed more than dog drool to do the trick. They needed—

"Jacuzzis," said Jo out loud. "Raymond, chase your tail."

Raymond didn't have to be told twice. Chasing his tail was his favorite hobby, second only to chasing mailmen.

He chased his tail right there on Mason Street. He darted in and out of the dinosaurs' legs, leaving behind Jacuzzi-size holes.

"Keep going, boy!" yelled Jo. "Chase your tail."

The dinosaurs slipped on the slobber and tripped in the Jacuzzi holes. Down they went. Jo joined in with a Knuckle Sandwich here and there.

Dinosaurs were shattering all over the place.

"No, no, no!" screamed Dr. Dastardly.

While the evil scientist was busy pulling his hair out, Jo ran over and snatched the Re-animator Laminator from his hands. She switched it to laminator mode, and before you could say "Dr. Dastardly and Pete were laminated," Dr. Dastardly and Pete were laminated.

Just like that.

Lofty Thoughts

Word soon got around about Jo Schmo, the superhero who saved San Francisco with the help of her drooling dog. The mayor, who had almost become dessert, called her up and told her how proud he was to have her helping out in the city.

So did the police chief.

Even Jo's teacher, Mrs. Freep, didn't mind anymore when Jo went on long bathroom breaks. She knew it probably had something to do with bank robbers or terrorists or mad scientists who

were up to no good. Or maybe Jo had had too much to drink and it was just a long bathroom break.

In any case, Mrs. Freep didn't care. She was just proud that Prairie Street Elementary School had a superhero to watch over things.

But the proudest person of all was Jo's mother. Once Dr. Dastardly and Pete were away in prison and all the bones were cleaned up on Mason Street, Mrs. Schmo baked a sponge cake to celebrate.

"Wow," she said, taking the cake out of the oven, "look how lofty it is!"

"Say that again," Jo said.

"Look at the sponge cake. Don't you think it's lofty?"

Jo looked at her grandfather, who was sitting at the kitchen table with the police radio to his ear. "Lofty?" said Jo.

"Lofty?" said Grandpa Joe.

Jo jumped to her feet. "That's it!" She tied her cape around her neck and ran outside. "Sponge cake!" she said in a loud voice.

And right then, she lifted off the ground.

"Sponge cake," she said again. She rose even further.

"Sponge cake," she said a third time. And before you could say "There goes the city," there *went* the city.

Jo flew over Chinatown, then North Beach, and then out over the water of the bay. She soared and

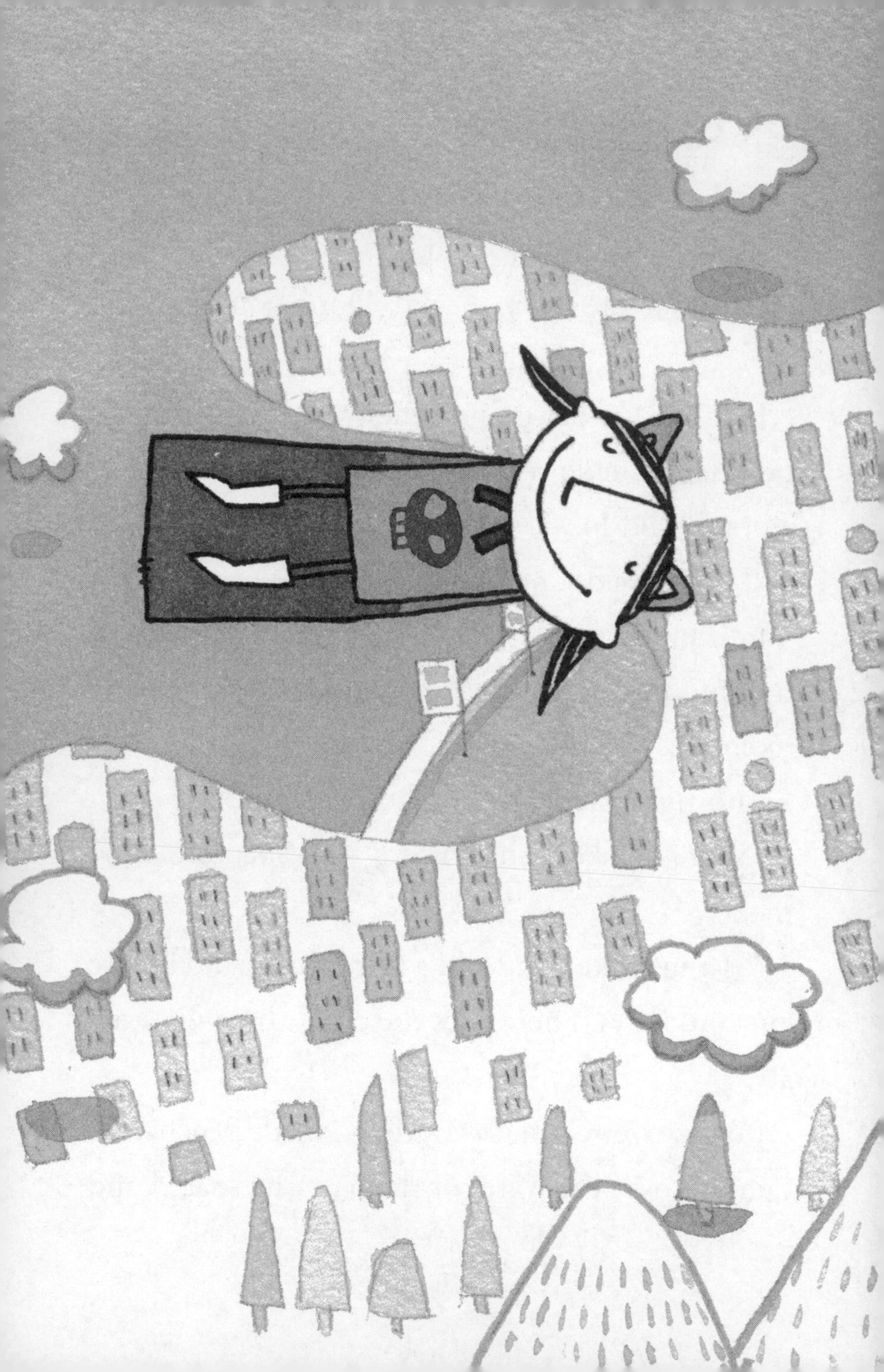

twirled, dipped and climbed. She was flying at last. Jo Schmo, Superhero, was flying.

She kept at it until the sun began to dip below the horizon; then she headed back to Crimshaw Avenue, landing lightly in the backyard, where Raymond was busy soaking in one of the four Jacuzzis.

He looked at her with an expression that said, "Can we catch some more bad guys tomorrow?"

"Absolutely," said Jo. "I love catching bad guys."

So did Raymond. He climbed out of the Jacuzzi, shook himself off, and then the two of them, superhero and sidekick, went inside.

Tomorrow there would be more problems to face in the city, more villains to catch, more crimes to stop, and Jo Schmo would be ready to face them. But for now, there was only one thing on her mind.

Sponge cake.

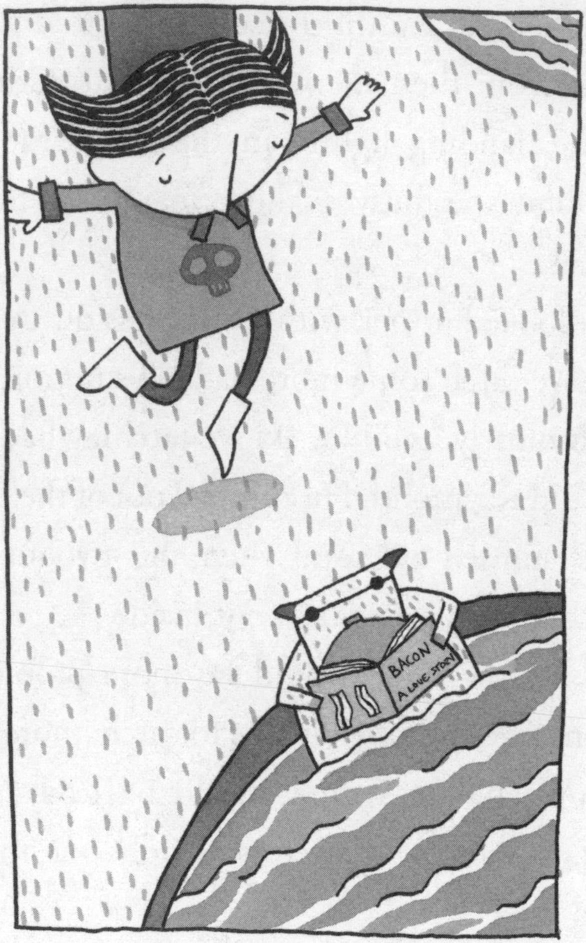
BACON
A LOVE STORY